This Little Tiger book belongs to:

*To the real Delphi, with much love, special girl ~ L G*

*For John, Laurie and James ~ P M*

LITTLE TIGER PRESS
An imprint of Magi Publications
1 The Coda Centre, 189 Munster Road, London SW6 6AW
www.littletigerpress.com

First published in Great Britain 2006
This edition published 2006

Text copyright © Magi Publications 2006
Illustrations copyright © Patricia MacCarthy 2006
Patricia MacCarthy has asserted her right to be identified as the illustrator
of this work under the Copyright, Designs and Patents Act, 1988

A CIP catalogue record for this book is available from the British Library

All rights reserved • ISBN 978-1-84506-260-6

Printed in Singapore

10 9 8 7 6 5 4 3 2

# The Tiniest Mermaid

Laura Garnham

*Illustrated by*

Patricia MacCarthy

LITTLE TIGER PRESS
London

Lily lived by the wide blue sea.
On summer nights she would sit on
the beach, gazing out over the waves,
dreaming of magic and adventure.

One night, as she sat by the rock pools, a faint sparkle caught her eye and a little voice cried out, "Help! Please help me!"

Lily gasped. It was a mermaid!
A beautiful, tiny mermaid! Was
she dreaming? But the mermaid
called out again, "Help me,
please! My tail was hurt in
the storm last night and
I can't get back home!"

"Oh, you poor thing!" said Lily, kneeling
by the rock pool. "I'll help you, if I can."
"Thank you," whispered the mermaid.
"You'll be safe with me," said Lily softly.
"I'll look after you."

Lily scooped the
delicate mermaid
from the water.
She walked carefully
up the steps, through
the house to her room.
By her bed was a huge
glass fish tank, the perfect
place for a mermaid to rest.
As she slipped into the water the tiny mermaid smiled.
"I'm Delphi. What's your name?"
"Lily," said Lily, smiling back at her new friend.

That night Lily sat up for a long time, watching over Delphi
as she slept. "I just knew mermaids were real," she whispered
to the fish. "Now you let her sleep and get better."

The next morning Lily leapt out of bed and rushed to the fish tank. Had it all been a dream? She stared anxiously through the glass and there, in the castle, was Delphi!

"You're still here!" Lily cried with delight.

"Of course," laughed Delphi. "Where else would I be?"

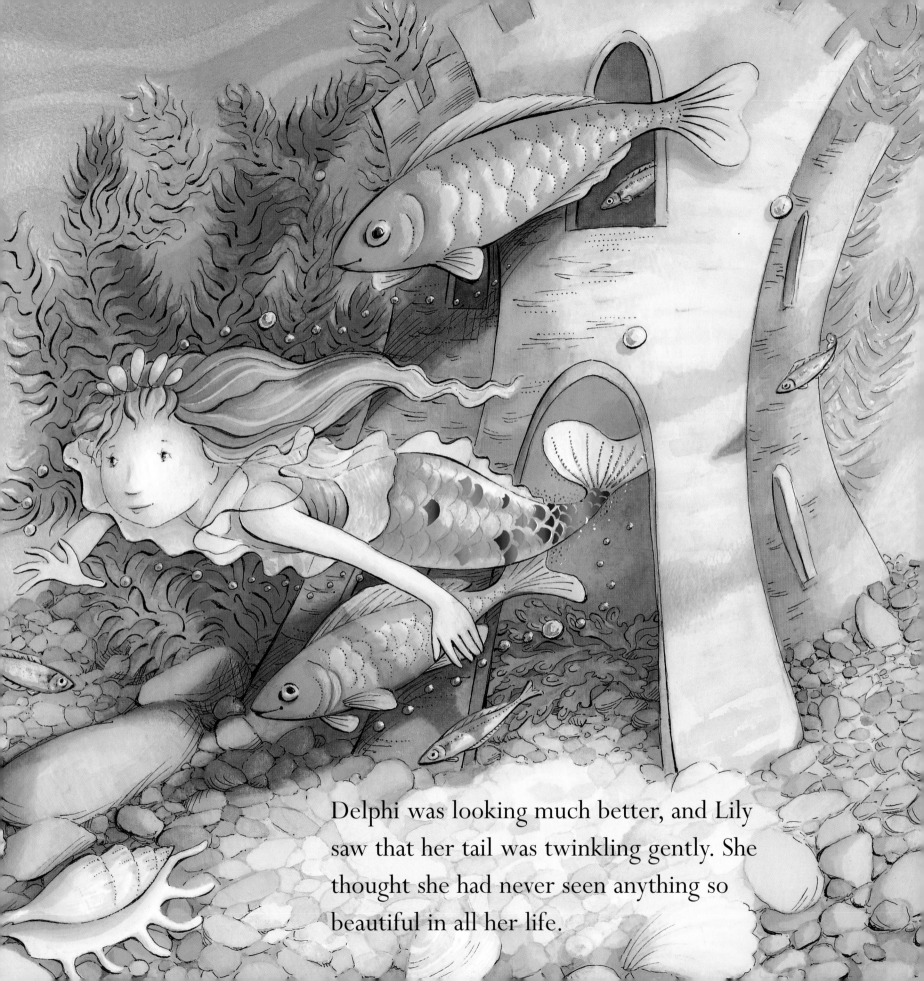

Delphi was looking much better, and Lily saw that her tail was twinkling gently. She thought she had never seen anything so beautiful in all her life.

Lily and Delphi talked all day. Delphi spoke of a world where mermaids swam through the coral, playing with sea horses. Lily could almost feel the water and see the light and colour of the ocean.

That night her dreams were filled with magic and mermaids and a special place far, far under the sea.

Slowly Delphi grew stronger. As her magic returned her tail sparkled brighter, and she transformed the tank into a shimmering underwater wonderland.

Lily raced home after school each day, and she and Delphi talked and talked until they were the best of friends.

"I wish I were a mermaid," said Lily one night.

"It is wonderful," Delphi said wistfully. "My friends and I travel the whole world using our magic to help trapped or hurt animals. And sometimes we use our sparkling tails to guide sailors home through terrible storms."

"Wow!" said Lily in wonder. "I never knew!"

"It's exciting, but it can be very scary," said Delphi.
"When I was hurt in that awful storm, I was separated
from my friends by a huge wave and thrown on to
the rocks." She sighed. "They must be wondering
what happened to me."

Lily gasped. Delphi's
friends would be so
worried about her!
"Oh Delphi," she cried.
"You must go back to
your friends!"
"Yes, I must," said Delphi.
"But I shall miss you."
"If only we didn't have
to say goodbye!" sighed Lily.
"I wish I could come with you.
Or just visit your magical world."
Delphi smiled suddenly. "I could show you, if you like.
Close your eyes . . ."
Lily took a deep breath as Delphi started singing a gentle,
lilting song. Lily could feel magic all round her and hear the rush
of the ocean growing louder . . .

All at once she was there with Delphi, swimming with dolphins as they danced and dived through the water.
Further and further they swam through the warm blue ocean until the setting sun turned the white beaches gold.

When Lily fell asleep that night she could still hear the whale's song and feel the sand between her toes.

The next morning Lily cradled Delphi in her hands
for the very last time as she carried her to the seashore.
   "Don't be sad, Lily," said Delphi softly, and she gave
her a special shell. "Whenever you miss me," she said,
"put the shell to your ear and you will hear the magic
of the sea whispering inside."

With a flick of her glittering tail, the tiny mermaid swam off. But as she waved goodbye Lily saw two more shining tails appear at Delphi's side. Delphi was with her friends and she was safe. And Lily knew that whenever she missed her she could listen to the sounds of the shell and look for the sparkles glimmering in the sea, for Delphi would always be near.

# Dive into a book from Little Tiger Press

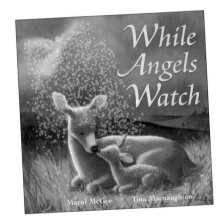

For information regarding any of the above titles
or for our catalogue, please contact us:
Little Tiger Press, 1 The Coda Centre,
189 Munster Road, London SW6 6AW
Tel: 020 7385 6333  Fax: 020 7385 7333
E-mail: info@littletiger.co.uk
www.littletigerpress.com